captain Cal

and the GREAT SPACE RACE

by Jan Dallimore

illustrated by Richard Morden

Picture Window Books
Minneapolis, Minnesota

First Published in the United States in 2010
by Picture Window Books
151 Good Counsel Drive
P.O. Box 669
Mankato, Minnesota 56002
www.picturewindowbooks.com

First published in Australia in 2007 by Black Dog Books
text copyright © Jan Dallimore 2007
illustrations copyright © Richard Morden 2007

Library of Congress Cataloging-in-Publication Data
Dallimore, Jan.
    Captain Cal and the Great Space Race / by Jan Dallimore ;
illustrated by Richard Morden.
       p. cm. — (Captain Cal)
       ISBN 978-1-4048-5508-3 (lib. bdg.)
       [1. Racing—Fiction. 2. Space ships—Fiction. 3. Interplanetary
voyages—Fiction. 4. Cheating—Fiction.] I. Morden, Richard, ill.
II. Title.
PZ7.D165Cao 2010
[Fic]—dc22
                                                          2008053799

Summary: Even though an Earth spaceship has never won the Great
Space Race, Captain Cal and the crew of the *Silver Pig* prepare to fly
into first place—without cheating.

Creative Director: Heather Kindseth
Graphic Designer: Bram Garvey

Printed in the United States of America

Table of Contents

Meet the crew of **The silver pig**

CAPTAIN CAL

CHIEF
NAVIGATOR
DAN

COPILOT
EBBY

Chapter 1
THE GREAT SPACE RACE

It was shaping up to be the most exciting day in space history for the crew of the *Silver Pig*. We were competing in the Great Space Race.

After seven days of competition, the race was down to three spaceships.

At 6 a.m. we had to meet with Chief Zordo. Chief Zordo was the main judge of the contest. It was his job to give us our map.

Two special galactic locations were marked on the map. We had to hunt for treasure at these locations.

I wanted to prove that I was the best pilot in the galaxy. If the *Silver Pig* won, it would be the first time an Earth spaceship took first place in the Great Space Race.

Chapter 2
STRAIGHT TO PLANET SPLAT

"Let's go, crew!" I said. "Dan, we need to go straight to Planet Splat to meet Chief Zordo."

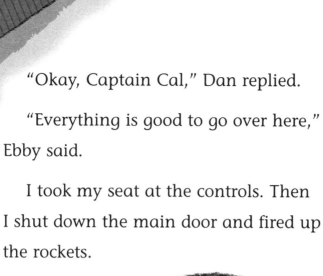

"Okay, Captain Cal," Dan replied.

"Everything is good to go over here," Ebby said.

I took my seat at the controls. Then I shut down the main door and fired up the rockets.

"We need to head for Grottsville, then take a sharp right to the Dog Star," said Dan, our navigator. "Hey, what's that behind the *Silver Pig*?"

"It looks like … it's *Big Red* from Mars," I said. "And here comes *Minus One* from Planet Zero. Increase the speed, Ebby," I ordered.

"Yes, Captain," she replied.

Chapter 3
THE RACE BEGINS

Captain Manta from Mars passed the *Silver Pig* at a frightening speed.

"He was the winner last year," said Dan.

"Well, that's last year's news," I said.

The three ships touched down within five micro-seconds of each other.

"Now we have to run to the summit. The first crew there will get their map and instructions first," I said.

We sprinted all the way.

Chief Zordo was waiting.

"Listen carefully," he said in a loud voice. "You must find the treasures and bring them back here before sunset. May the best ship win!"

We raced back to our ship and jumped on board.

"Dan, as chief navigator you will be in charge of getting us from one place to the other in the quickest possible time," I said.

Dan nodded. "You can count on me, Captain Cal," he said.

Ebby was in charge of looking after the treasures once we found them.

"I'll put them in the safe," she said.

Chapter 4
FIRST STOP: MARS

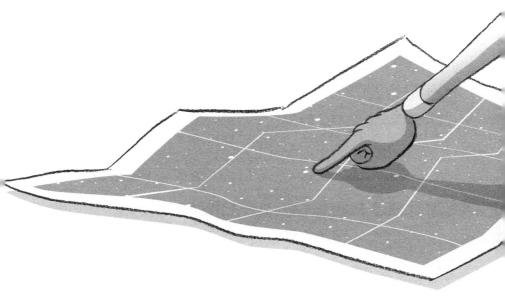

"Our first stop is Mars," said Dan. "Travel east past the Yellow Star, then turn right past Saturn. Mars will be straight ahead."

"Thanks, Dan. Increasing speed now," I said.

Ebby was busy reading the race map. "We have to find the biggest crater on Mars and then look for a blue flag. Our first clue will be on the flag," she said.

The *Silver Pig* was the first spaceship to land on Mars. *Minus One,* with Captain Nort and his crew, was right behind us.

"Let's go, crew," I yelled.

Suddenly Captain Manta and his crew flew past us in three mini capsules and disappeared over the hill.

"Hey! That's cheating," said Ebby.

"Keep going," I yelled. "We're almost there."

"What's that stuff covering the
ground?" Dan asked.

"It's ice!" I yelled.

But it was too late. Everyone was
slipping and crashing into each other.
No one could stand up.

"It never snows on Mars," said Ebby.
"What's going on?"

"It's an obstacle made by the race organizers," I said.

Captain Manta couldn't land his capsules on the ice.

"Come on, crew! This is our chance!" I yelled.

The tree of us rolled down to the bottom of Humungus, the biggest crater on Mars.

Chapter 5
BREAKING THE RULES

I crawled toward the flag, but as I reached for it, Captain Manta flew overhead and grabbed it.

"Hey, he took our flag!" Ebby yelled.

Captain Manta had broken all the rules. Luckily, a piece of paper with the clue was lying on the ground. It read: *Go directly to the center of Humungus, face the Blue Star, and dig. Good luck.*

We rushed to the center of the crater and found a tiny rainbow-colored stone under the red dust. Ebby popped it into the safe. Then we raced back to the ship.

The *Minus One* team was catching up. The *Big Red* team had already left.

"We have to stop evil Captain Manta," I told the crew.

"But how, Captain Cal?" asked Ebby.

"I'm not sure," I said.

Chapter 6

PLAYING DIRTY

The three spaceships were heading to Earth to find the next treasure. I noticed that it was getting hard to see.

"Ebby, can you check the weather dial?" I asked.

"I can see a huge dust storm heading this way, Captain," she replied.

"What do we do now?" Dan asked.

"We'll have to fly on autopilot," I said. "Where did *Minus One* go?"

"It disappeared off the radar," Ebby
called out.

"It looks like Captain Nort's out of the
race," Dan said.

Suddenly *Big Red* appeared in front of
the *Silver Pig,* blocking our flight path.

"That's it! I've had enough of that big bully!" I yelled. "I'm going to stop Manta once and for all."

I turned on the strong jets, the blinking lights, and the laser beams.

"Let's see what he does with that," I said.

Big Red shot upward to escape our beams. Then it dropped down on our left side.

A voice boomed over a loudspeaker. "Listen, kid, go home! Only the best pilot can win this race. And that's me," said Captain Manta.

"That does it," I said. "I'll show him who's the best pilot. Hang on, everyone. I'm pulling every bit of power from the *Silver Pig*. Buckle up those space belts. Here we go!"

Chapter 7
TREASURE HUNT

"Go straight to the Great Trass Pyramid in Egypt," said Dan.

"The clue is a riddle this time," said Ebby. "The treasure is a slippery creature. It lives in hidden places, and its name rhymes with cake and bake."

"It has to be a snake!" Dan said.

"You're so smart, Dan," Ebby replied.

We had beaten *Big Red* to the Great
Trass Pyramid, but it wasn't far behind.

"We need to find this treasure in the next few minutes, or we can kiss this race good-bye," I said.

We ran around the pyramid looking for our next clue.

"There's a basket," Dan said.

I opened the basket lid. Inside was the tiniest snake I'd ever seen.

"It's so cute," Ebby said as she popped it into the safe.

"Quick, back to the *Silver Pig*," I said.

Just then Captain Manta raced over. "Give me whatever you've got in that basket," he demanded.

Ebby shrugged and handed over the basket.

Captain Manta reached into the basket as we raced back to our spaceship.

"Hey! Wait!" he yelled. "There's nothing in here."

"Find your own treasure, Manta," I yelled back as we closed the space door.

Chapter 8
AND THE WINNER IS . . .

The *Silver Pig* took off, zooming toward Planet Splat. It had reached full power.

"We're close now, Captain Cal," said Dan.

"The *Silver Pig* and my great crew have done it!" I said. "Wait until everyone finds out that we're the top astronauts in the galaxy!"

"Here comes *Big Red*," Dan yelled. "Go to the right of the Purple Star. It's the quickest path."

I pushed all the power levers and buttons. The ship accelerated to full power. It shook. It rolled. But it kept going faster and faster.

"I can see Planet Splat now. Prepare to land," I said.

Big Red was getting farther behind. "They've run out of fuel. It serves them right for cheating," said Dan.

Soon *Big Red* was just a dot in outer space.

"Look! There's a huge crowd down there," said Ebby.

"And TV cameras," said Dan.

"I hope there's food," I said.

We jumped to the ground and took our treasures to Chief Zordo. He handed them over to the officials, who approved them.

"Let me present you with the Gold Galaxy Cup and medals from the Greater Galactic Committee," Chief Zordo said. "You truly are the greatest pilot in the galaxy, Captain Cal."

Everyone cheered.

"I am the greatest pilot in the galaxy,"
I agreed. "But only because I have the
best ship and the greatest crew."

And everyone agreed.

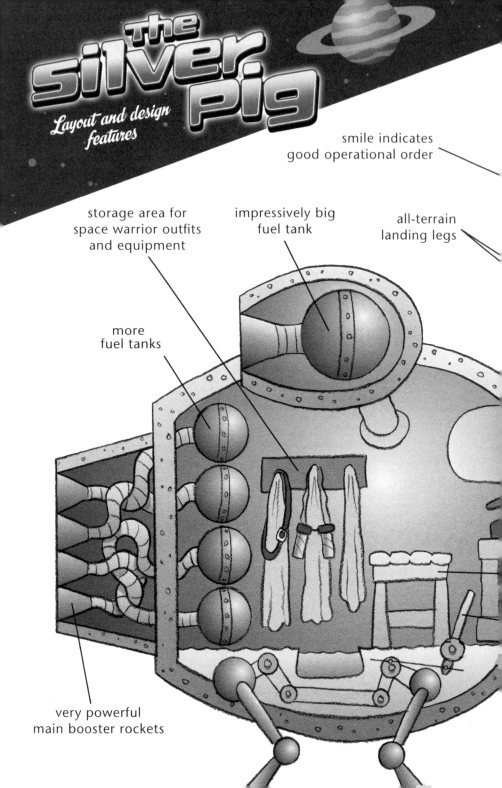

The silver Pig

Layout and design features

smile indicates
good operational order

storage area for
space warrior outfits
and equipment

impressively big
fuel tank

all-terrain
landing legs

more
fuel tanks

very powerful
main booster rockets

heat-proof
view port

secondary
rockets

stunning array of controls
and technical-looking stuff

a door for getting in
and keeping space out

food detector and
navigational gears

bench seat for three

little lever for
lowering landing legs

space tourism:
Not Just a Dream

Space tourists train for about a year before going into space.

Dennis Tito was the first space tourist. He paid $20 million for a trip into space in 2001.

Anousheh Ansari, an Iranian-American scientist, was the first female space tourist in 2006.

Many space tourists work on science experiments on their journey.

The first space tourists reached space in
Russian rockets. Private companies are
looking to fund future space tourism.

One company is even trying to build a
space hotel. When the hotel reaches orbit,
its rooms will inflate like balloons.

The first space tourists went to the
International Space Station. In the future,
tourists might travel to the Moon or stay
in a space hotel.

ABOUT THE AUTHOR

Jan Dallimore loves writing books for children. Her first book was *Granny: Survivor*. Jan finds writing relaxing and would much rather write than cook or clean. Jan's dog, Beau, sits under her feet while she writes. If Jan wasn't a writer, she would be a world traveler.

ABOUT THE ILLUSTRATOR

Richard Morden has illustrated picture books, textbooks, children's encyclopedias, book covers, posters, and more. His first picture book, *Ziggy & Zrk and the Meteor of Doom,* received the 2005 Crichton Award for Children's Book Illustration. Richard's highly developed digital skills and his love of science fiction have helped him create memorable characters and creative images.

GLOSSARY

accelerated (ak-SEL-uh-rate-id)—sped up or moved faster

competition (kom-puh-TISH-uhn)—a contest

crater (KRAY-tur)—a large hole caused by a big object crashing into the ground

galaxy (GAL-uhk-see)—a large group of stars and planets

navigator (NAV-uh-gate-ur)—the person who guides the trip

obstacle (OB-stuh-kuhl)—something that gets in the way of completing a task

pilot (PYE-luht)—the person who flies the aircraft

summit (SUHM-it)—the highest point

DISCUSSION QUESTIONS

1. Captain Cal is the pilot of the *Silver Pig*. Would you want to be a pilot? Discuss your reasons.

2. Captain Manta does not follow the rules of the race. He is caught cheating many different times. Why do you think people cheat?

3. The *Silver Pig*, *Big Red*, and *Minus One* are the three spaceships competing in the race. What would you name a spaceship? Why?

WRITING PROMPTS

1. What kind of race would you like to compete in? Name your race, write a race description, and make a list of at least five rules for your race.

2. The big race starts on Planet Splat. Make up a new planet. Create a name and a description for it. Draw a picture of your planet as well.

3. Captain Cal and his crew win the big race. Write a small newspaper story covering the big event.